TOMMY TABLET AT NIAGARA FALLS

WRITTEN BY **Julie Prantera**

ILLUSTRATED BY **Kevin Finkbeiner**

credo
house publishers

To Mason,
Keep Reading ♡
Mrs. Julie
Prantera
2021

Published in the United States by Credo House Publishers,
a division of Credo Communications LLC, Grand Rapids, Michigan
www.credohousepublishers.com

ISBN-13: 978-1-625860-64-4

Printed in the United States of America

To my sweet nephew, Nathan.

With much love, Aunt Julie

Tommy was tucked in with all the other tablets hoping to be picked for an exciting adventure. *Pick me. Oh please, pick me!* Tommy thought as he waited and waited.

Tommy knew he was not like the other tablets.
He **loved** to travel. He wanted to see the world.
Tommy longed for a family that would take him
to tour and explore new places.

Sweet Nathanael went to school to check out a tablet. His teacher reached for #11. Tommy wanted to leap for joy. He felt like the luckiest tablet on earth. Little did Nathan know that #11, also known as Tommy, had a passion for children, adventure, and **life**.

Nathan placed the tablet into his spider backpack. Tommy could smell Nathan's lunch in the cozy space. *Yum, that smells so good,* Tommy thought. He wanted to ask, *Where are we going?* **What will it be like?** Tommy just could not wait. Nathan had a spring in his step as he prepared to depart.

When Nathan's daddy was ready for their adventure he said, "Everybody buckled up?" Nathan replied, "Roll out." It was their fun family tradition.

Nathan, who was super six, loved traveling with his tablet companion. He enjoyed movies, games, and activities along the way. Tommy enjoyed the time together.

Nathan frequently asked his parents, ***"Are we there yet?"***

Meanwhile, Tommy was getting sleepy. He had hoped to feel recharged soon.

Both Nathan and Tommy enjoyed a snooze as they traveled the highways. Hours had passed. After a refreshing snack, Nathan woke up Tommy. He was planning to watch one of his favorite movies. It was about a puppet that wanted to be a **real boy**. Tommy could relate to the puppet as he had some of those same feelings.

Tommy could tell that something was about to happen. As they pulled off the highway, Nathan's daddy said, **"Put your shoes on."**

Nathan knew that was his signal that they would soon be there. Tommy could barely contain himself and thought, *Where are we?* Then he heard a very loud sound. Nathan said, "Mama, is that it? Is that what we came all this way to see?" Excitement **filled** the air.

The family jumped out of the van. Nathan reached back for Tommy knowing he would help to capture their **memories** with his camera. Nathan's mommy grabbed his hand as they walked down the steep hill to their destination. Many people had come to see it too. Tommy and Nathan both knew that this must be a very special place.

As they got closer, the sound became louder and **louder**. Tommy could not believe his eyes. Both Nathan and Tommy were still as they saw Niagara Falls for the very first time. The water was **rushing** over the rocks. It took Nathan's breath away.

He **squeezed** his daddy's hand with excitement.

Nathan tapped on Tommy's tummy. He was **excited** and was searching for Tommy's camera. Nathan started capturing the Falls one picture at a time. It was magnificent and both Tommy and Nathan wanted to remember it forever. *Snap, Snap, Snap!*

"Mama, it is so beautiful," Nathan said with great **joy**. Tommy was so pleased to see Nathan so excited. Tommy knew the pictures would be great. He was thrilled that they could be shared with friends back at school. Tommy felt proud that he could help Nathan capture all these beautiful images.

Tommy never dreamed he would ever see something like this. He, too, admired the pictures along the way. Tommy thought, *How could it be? Who could have created such a beautiful sight?* Nathan knew who had created it. He and his mother had talked about **God's beautiful handiwork** around the world.

The water kept coming. Tommy wondered if the water was always flowing. He wanted to ask if the water ever stopped. Nathan was wondering too. He asked his dad, "Does the water ever **freeze?**" Nathan's daddy said, "Part of the water does freeze. The rushing of the water helps to keep it flowing most of the time." That was a BIG question for such a young explorer.

Tommy was proud of his friend.

Tommy and Nathan
were both thinking,
I just can't believe it.
It was very exciting
for them both.

Nathan took more exciting pictures to **share**.

Tommy began to imagine traveling in a barrel over the waterfalls. *Oh, what an exciting trip it would be*, Tommy thought. He wished he could tell Nathan how he was feeling. He knew Nathan would want to **go** too.

Nathan asked his mama, "Did you get to come
to Niagara Falls when you were a little girl?"
His mother shook her head no. Nathan knew
this was a very **special** trip.

Nathan wrapped his arms around his mother
to give her a **giant** hug. Nathan loved his mother
very much. His daddy captured the hug with
#11's video camera.

It was one of Tommy's **favorite** moments from
their trip together. He wished he could join in and
make it a big group hug.

There were a lot of people looking at the waterfalls. Everyone seemed so happy. Tommy wondered if it was the **prettiest place on earth**. The time together made him feel like he was a part of the family.

Nathan heard his mother say, "It is time to head
to our hotel." Nathan snapped one last shot as they
headed back up the hill. Tommy looked back at
Niagara Falls as Nathan carried him away. It was
a **memory** he never wanted to forget.

After reaching the hotel, the family settled in
for swimming and fun.

Tommy was put to bed.
He knew Nathan's family
needed time together.
He had grown to **love** them.

Tommy also needed to feel
recharged after the long day.

The next day, as the family packed up for the long trip home, Tommy felt thankful. He was so glad that the teacher had picked him for this adventure. The family headed to the Falls to see it one last time. They piled out of the car leaving Tommy behind. The tablet **peeked** out the window and saw someone taking the family's photo in front of the beautiful waterfalls. Tommy was happy for Nathan and his parents.

He looked forward to spending time with his new
friend on the long ride home. Tommy wished he
could tell Nathan what a good friend he had been.
He was hoping that one day they could travel
together again. Tommy wanted to give him a hug
and say, **"Keep in touch."** Tablet #11 would soon
be put back on the school's cart.

Tommy was thinking, ***"Where will my next
adventure take me?"***

Will Tommy's daydream come true?

To be continued . . .

Author's Acknowledgments

I could not have done this work without the love and support of my husband, children, parents, brother, and in-laws. You all mean the world to me.

Karen Carpio, thank you for graciously sharing your beautiful photographs with me.

Nathan, thank you for being so sweet and for inspiring Aunt Julie to be adventuresome like you.

Tara McFarland and Ann Klein, thank you for your friendship, encouragement, and editing skills.

My greatest appreciation goes to my former student, Kevin Finkbeiner, for his delightful illustrations and giving spirit. Your kindness and dedication is greatly appreciated. It has been my pleasure to partner with you on this endeavor. Your talent is an amazing gift. I pray that this work opens many doors for you. I cannot thank you enough.

AUTHOR: **Julie Prantera**

Tommy Tablet at Niagara Falls is Julie's premier book. As the elementary technology teacher at Oakland Christian School, Julie is passionate about encouraging children to use technology to enjoy life's adventures. She wants to help instill a lifelong love of reading to each child she encounters. She is currently working on a new Tommy Tablet adventure and taking her books to a digital format.

Julie has a degree in journalism, is a certified teacher (K-8), and has her master's degree in elementary teaching. Adding author to her business card has always been a dream. Julie resides in Oxford, Michigan, with her husband, Guy. They have three grown children, Joshua, Austin, and Tiffany. Julie is honored to introduce her former student, Kevin Finkbeiner. His talent brings life to Tommy Tablet.

ILLUSTRATOR: **Kevin Finkbeiner**

Kevin has been bringing his wild creativity to life ever since he taught himself to draw at the age of five. He loves to use his work to make people laugh, crack a smile, and most importantly, tell a good story. His interests include other artistic areas like writing, animation, and film.

In 2014 he graduated from the Motion Picture Institute in Troy, Michigan, with a degree in film production. He currently resides in Orange County, California, working on assorted projects and continuing to build a long and fruitful career.

touch to open.

2:45p

Tommytablet.com